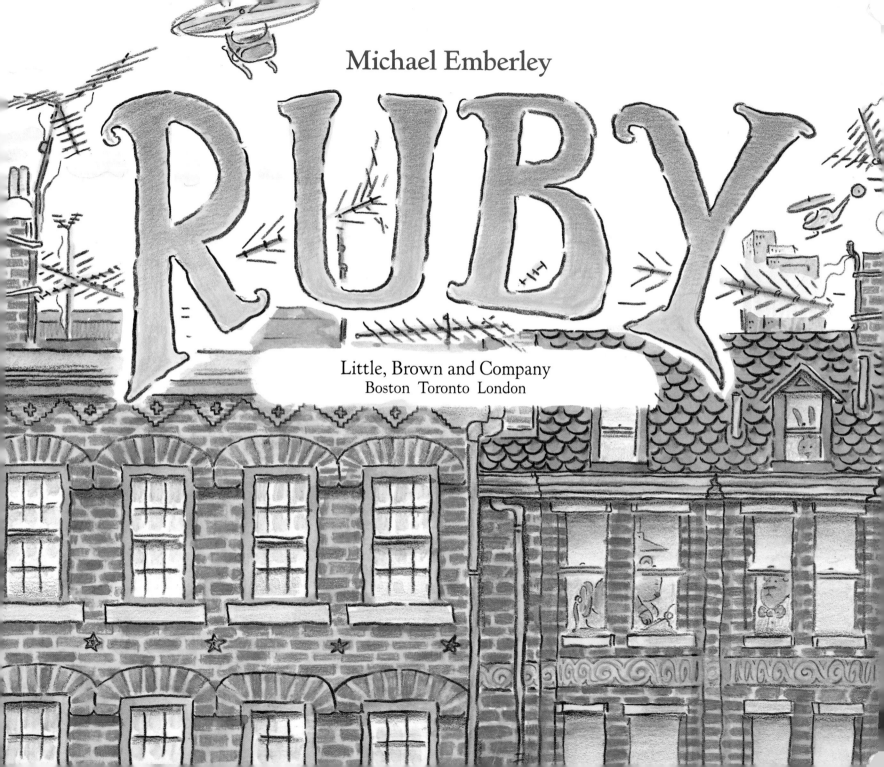

Michael Emberley

RUBY

Little, Brown and Company
Boston Toronto London

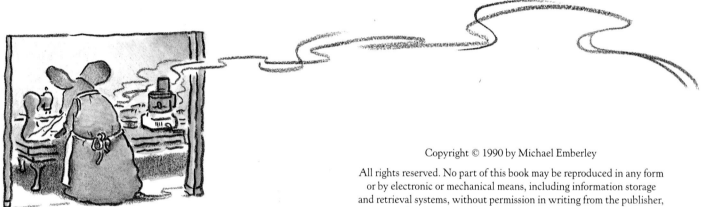

ALSO BY MICHAEL EMBERLEY

Dinosaurs! A Drawing Book

More Dinosaurs! And Other Prehistoric Beasts:
A Drawing Book

The Sports Equipment Book

First Paperback Edition

Library of Congress Cataloging-in-Publication Data
Emberley, Michael.
  Ruby / Michael Emberley.
    p.   cm.
  Summary: While taking cheese pies to her Granny, Ruby, a small but
tough-minded little mouse, forgets her mother's advice not to talk to
cats.
  ISBN 0-316-23643-8 (hc)
  ISBN 0-316-23660-8 (pb)
  [1. Mice — Fiction. 2. Cats — Fiction.] I. Title.
PZ7.E566Ru 1990   89-12108
[E] — dc20

10 9 8 7 6 5 4 3 2
WOR
Published simultaneously in Canada
by Little, Brown & Company (Canada) Limited

Printed in the United States of America

Ruby's whiskers twitched. Out in the kitchen, Ruby's mother was just finishing a batch of her famous triple-cheese pies.

"Ruby!" her mother called.

"Yeah?" said Ruby.

"I'd like you to go over to your granny's this afternoon."

"But, Ma . . ." Ruby groaned.

"She's not feeling too well," said her mother.

"But . . ."

"Now I've put in a couple of pies for each of you, plus a few extra in case Granny's neighbor Mrs. Mastiff stops by. You remember Mrs. Mastiff, don't you, Ruby?"

"Sure, Ma," Ruby mumbled.

"Now I want you to go straight there," her mother warned. "No talking to strangers, especially cats. Do you hear me, Ruby? Never, never trust a cat."

"Never, never, never," said Ruby flatly.

"And please don't read as you walk," called her mother. "You'll walk right in front of a bus one of these days."

"OK, Ma," grumbled Ruby.

Ruby got as far as the corner before she forgot her mother's advice and pulled out her book. A few paragraphs later . . .

KA-PUMPH!
"Hey, kid, what's the rush?"

Ruby looked up. She had run into a grimy-looking reptile whose hot breath smelled very much like dirty gym socks.

"Buzz off, barf breath," Ruby replied, forgetting more of her mother's advice.

"Smart-mouth twerp," grunted the grimy reptile. "What's in the bag?"
"None of your beeswax, creepo," snapped Ruby, trying not to breathe.
The creature's odor was so foul, Ruby's whiskers began to wilt.

"You better watch your yap, rodent," hissed the reptile. "Or I might tie
your scrawny tail to a brick and take you for a swim."
"Right," snorted Ruby. "And you can't even tie your own shoes."

The grimy reptile turned an alarming shade of purple. Its eyes narrowed to slits. Its forked tongue flicked in and out. Instinctively, Ruby took a step backward. But suddenly a grimy claw shot out and snatched the cheese pies.

"YOW!" shrieked Ruby.

"Put a cork in it, rodent!" spat the grimy reptile.

Then, as he turned to make his escape, an extremely well-dressed stranger appeared out of nowhere, stopping the thief in his tracks.

"Is there a problem here?" said the stranger casually in a smooth, velvety voice.

Ruby was speechless. The grimy reptile spluttered. "What the . . .
ack . . . what is that stuff?"

"Just some warm soapy water," said the stranger. "Now what do you
say, my scaly friend? Why don't you find your way back to whatever
dark hole you crawled out of?" He paused to show some teeth. "Or
perhaps you would enjoy another long overdue bath?"

The grimy reptile glared at them. Then, deciding to stay dry and dirty, he slithered off, muttering foul curses.

"I hope that you are all right, my dear," purred the stranger, turning to Ruby.

"Yes, thank you," said Ruby politely. His breath smelled like cat food mixed with cheap peppermint mouthwash.

"You know," purred the stranger, "a tender, er, pretty thing like you really shouldn't be strolling the streets alone. You never know what nasty creatures may be prowling the dark alleys. I say, I would find it a great pleasure if you would allow me to escort you for the remainder of your journey today."

"Um . . . I don't think so," said Ruby, watching a bead of drool slip down a whisker.

"I beg you to reconsider," persisted the stranger.

"I'm only going to have tea with my granny and a neighbor," said Ruby. "I think I can make it."

"Really? Well, just where do Granny and this, um, neighbor live?" purred the stranger.

Ruby squinted at the stranger a moment. Then she answered slowly, "She has an apartment right at the top of Beacon Hill, number thirty-four."

"Yes," said the stranger, smiling warmly. "I know the neighborhood."

"Well," said Ruby, "if you'll excuse me, I should call Granny. She'll be worried if I'm late, so —"

But the stranger was not listening. He waved for a taxi. "Please be careful," he said as he got in. "You won't find a friendly face like mine around every corner. And I certainly wouldn't want anything to happen to you."

"I'll bet you wouldn't," mumbled Ruby as the taxi pulled away. She then went over to a pay phone and made her call. When she had hung up, the taxi and the stranger had disappeared into the noisy city traffic.

"Where to?" grunted the taxi driver.

"Thirty-four Beacon Street," said the cat. "And step on it."

The cat couldn't help chuckling to himself. "What a wonderfully stupid child. Now I'll have *three* mice for lunch instead of one! I'll be there long before that tender little morsel. Plenty of time to nibble on the other two old rodents as appetizers." He giggled. "How clever I am!" He giggled again. "How wonderfully, wickedly clever!"

The cat arrived and rang the bell at number thirty-four. "Who is it?" asked a deep voice on the intercom.

"It's me," squeaked the cat, "little Ruby. I have some goodies for you."

"Ruby?" said the voice. "Just a minute."

"I hope Granny has some tarragon," thought the cat. "Tarragon is just the thing to have with roast mouse."

"You can come in now," sang the voice.

"Yum, yum," said the cat, as he quickly slipped inside.

Before long, Ruby arrived at number thirty-four nearly worn out from carrying all those cheese pies halfway across town and up Beacon Hill. She rang Granny's bell.

"Hello, Ruby dear," said a rough, squeaky voice.

"Granny? How did you know it was me?"

"I was expecting you, dear."

"You sound funny, Granny."

"It's just my cold, dear," said the voice. "Come on up."

Ruby was just reaching for the doorknob when suddenly . . .
the door swung open.

"Hi, Mrs. Mastiff," said Ruby.

"Hello, Ruby dear," said Mrs. Mastiff in her deep, cultured voice. "It was wise of you to call me instead of your granny. You were quite correct. That cat did show up here not long after your call. Doing a rather bad imitation of you, I must say."

"So, where's the slimebag now?" said Ruby.

"Oh, he's . . . gone," said Mrs. Mastiff, burping softly. "I imagine that I was not at all what he was expecting." An impish grin curled her mouth, making her look for a moment like a young pup.

Ruby gave Mrs. Mastiff a long look. "New hat?" she said finally.
"Why, yes," said Mrs. Mastiff, posing. "I just got it."
"Mmmm," said Ruby.

"What's all this?" said Granny, wobbling down the stairs.

"Hi, Granny," said Ruby.

"What? Oh, hello there, honey," said Granny.

"I've brought some of Ma's triple-cheese pies for tea," said Ruby.

"Hot dog! Oh! Sorry, Edna," said Granny, eyeing Mrs. Mastiff. "Didn't see you there. Well, let's get upstairs and dig in, I'm starved. Coming, Edna?"

"Thank you, but . . . I've just eaten," said Mrs. Mastiff.

"Suit yourself," said Granny, starting the long trip back up the stairs. "Phew! Does it stink of cat around here or is it just me? Better get upstairs, Ruby. Can't be too careful. Never trust a cat, I always say."

"Never, never, never," said Ruby.

FInC